All About ZAC!

By Michael-Anne Johns

SCHOLASTIC INC.

New York   Toronto   London   Auckland   Sydney
Mexico City   New Delhi   Hong Kong   Buenos Aires

ISBN-13: 978-0-545-114114-1

ISBN-10: 0-545-11414-4

© Scholastic, 2009

Published by Scholastic Inc.

SCHOLASTIC and associated logos are trademarks and/or registered trademarks of Scholastic Inc.

9 10 11 12/0

12 11 10 9 8 7 6 5 4 3 2 1

Designed by Deena Fleming

Printed in the U.S.A.

First printing, April 2009

Table of Contents

ZAC ATTACK!

THIS BOOK IS DEDICATED TO ALL YOU SUPER ZAC EFRON FANS—OLD AND NEW, AND EVEN FUTURE ONES.

Zac-mania began when he was just a toddler back in his hometown of Arroyo Grande, CA, and his parents, David and Starla Efron, first noticed that music was in his blood. "After watching *The Wizard of Oz* we found him emulating the Tin Man dance," David recalls. "Over time we noticed that he had an uncanny ability to listen to a song on the radio, memorize the lyrics, and sing it back a cappella with correct rhythm, tone, pitch, and inflection."

But over the years, the Efrons learned Zac had many more talents. When the rest of the world really recognized it with *High School Musical*, there was no stopping Zac. Yet with all the fame and fortune, glitter and glory that's been heaped on him, Zac's still the same down-to-earth guy who scraped his knees on his skateboard and played baseball "just so-so" back in the day! Actually Zac is proud of that fact and says, "I don't like cocky people. I'm such a regular dude. This whole [celebrity] thing is kind of awkward for me. I feel like the kid that snuck into some party and shouldn't be there.'"

WELL, WE'RE GLAD ZAC'S AT THIS PARTICULAR PARTY, SO LET'S GET READY TO HAVE A GOOD TIME. READ ON!

ZAC TAKES YOUR QUESTIONS
THE ULTIMATE Q&A

When did you first know that acting was what you wanted to do?

Zac: There was really a point where I sat down and said I wanted to be an actor. It was really just a culmination of events that just sort of led me here and now, looking back, I can't really put a finger on the spot where I said I want to do this for the rest of my life.

Did you take drama classes?

Zac: Yeah, that is definitely what sparked my interest. I did musical theater in our community. I did lots of plays in Santa Marina, all the community theater playhouses, and eventually I did a drama class in eighth grade. My teacher had an agent in Los Angeles and she recommended me to go down and meet him.

Have you sung all your life?

Zac: Well, yeah, musical theater was something that I naturally seemed to get into. I was also playing piano back then, so getting a little music under my belt couldn't hurt.

Are you grateful to your parents for suggesting you get into musical theater?

Zac: Yes! When I was younger, I was just always singing in the car, singing to the radio, and I don't know . . . maybe they got sick of hearing me do it only in the car?!!!

Do they have musical theater roots?

Zac: No. My parents are very far removed from the entertainment industry all together. They weren't performers or singers.

What was the best part of making the *High School Musical* movies?

Zac: Probably just hanging out with everyone on set. I made so many friends.

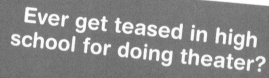

Ever get teased in high school for doing theater?

Zac: I was not a drama kid in high school. Most of my theater was in a professional community theater. I didn't do it in the high school. Looking back though maybe I should have.

Did you know any of the cast before?

Zac: Yeah, I knew Ashley, and she's probably the only one out of the cast I knew. But we all built amazing relationships. We remained best friends coming out of it.

What is it like being part of the Disney family early on?

Zac: I think more of the kids that come on to the Disney Channel [than any place else]. The Disney Channel does a good job of picking good kids, and I think maybe other places let a few slip by. I give everyone in *HSM* credit, and we didn't make it too over the top, which could have been a downfall. We made it more realistic, and I think it reached a larger audience and more people could relate.

Do you prefer movies to TV series?

Zac: I think my favorite is probably always going to be theater, but then again with theater your audience is limited to 600 people. Being on film you get to reach a much wider audience. It's great to know the number of people you're reaching is just phenomenal, so there're benefits to both. But I think filming a movie is a lot less stressful than being out in front of an audience. But it's also less rewarding, because you don't get to hear the immediate reaction of them clapping or the shouts or the laughter. You have to wait six months and then watch it with your brother and sister, and see how they like it. There are benefits to both.

Do you remember what your favorite book was when you were a little boy?

Zac: I loved the *Captain Underpants* novels and the *Goosebumps* and *Hank the Cowdog* series.

Is there a book that influenced you to learn more about a certain subject?

Zac: *Robinson Crusoe* was a good book I read and so was *1984*. . . . One of the early books I read in high school was *Frankenstein*. I remember not being excited to read after school, but when I started that book I didn't put it down. That was the first time I really got wrapped up in a story. I value that. And it really kept me going, all through the rest of the novels I read in school.

Why is reading important?

Zac: In a few pages of a book you can find ten times as much detail as a movie or a TV show can show you. It reveals the smallest and most important details in a scene or in a moment. Reading can open you to a much more descriptive or intimate scene than movies or TV.

What was your favorite subject in school?

Zac: English by far—I always did great in English. I was good at math too, but then one year, out of nowhere, math got hard. It was trigonometry and the second semester my brain melted. But that was when I was driving back and forth to . . . Los Angeles for work, so I was only showing up to school two to three days at a time. I was still getting all A's, but . . . I couldn't keep up. You need to keep up and have one-on-one with the teacher to do well in math.

If you could invite three people to dinner who would they be and where would you go or cook?

Zac: I would invite my hero when I was little from *The Terminator* and action movies, so Arnold Schwarzenegger, George Clooney, and Brad Pitt. I think they'd be a fun crowd and we would go to McDonalds and sit at one of the plastic tables.

Do you have a big fear?

Zac: Sharks, even though I surf, sharks are still a fear of mine. I'm scared of freaky things like *The Ring* and *The Grudge*. I have never been so scared in my entire life than when I sat and watched those movies. Even though it's unrealistic, it's scary.

Are there other projects out there that you want to do?

Zac: We'll see. I love *High School Musical*, but there are so many projects out there that I want to be a part of, so many genres that I want to try.

Do you have any favorite musicals?

Zac: Sure. One of my favorite musicals is actually a movie musical. Gene Kelly's *Singin' in the Rain* is a great one for me. A new one of my favorites is *Footloose*, of course. I love so many of them and I've been a part of so many great musicals. It's a crazy part of my life that I love.

Since you are famous now, do you have to be careful how you lead your life?

Zac: Slightly more careful. It's not that I have to be careful, but it's getting used to people observing my daily activities. Formerly, it was people would see the work, but now it's like I'll be at the grocery store buying Cheetos and there'll be people who are interested in that! It's funny.

What's your exercise regimen if you have one?

Zac: I don't know if I have a regimen. I just like to stay active. When I was young, I was always outside and playing sports. There're better things to do than sitting on the couch, I figure. I love hiking and if it gets me outside, if it gets me moving, then I love doing it. Sometimes the most convenient way to be active is going to the gym.

It's hard to eat healthy while on the set—what do you like from craft service table?

Zac: That's how I survive! I eat everything, whatever they have. Nuts, chips, fruit. And there're fresh Krispy Kremes every day!

If you had to choose going to the exclusive Hollywood eatery The Ivy and a fast food place, which would it be?

Zac: Quiznos! I can get an equally good sandwich at Quiznos: the honey mustard chicken sandwich with bacon on whole wheat. It's pretty cheap. If I buy a foot-long sandwich, it's like two meals.

Always being recognized—is it ever a problem?

Zac: I don't think it's a problem. Being recognized is fun. I don't think it can weigh you down unless you're having a private moment or you're having a really bad day.

Do you ever fear being considered just a teen musical idol?

Zac: I love doing musicals—don't get me wrong. But I'm an actor at heart. I'd like to try more adventurous roles. The last thing I want to do at the moment is straight teen movies. . . . It's really easy to worry about being pigeonholed in teen stardom. But if I stayed up at night worrying about that, I wouldn't be giving 110% in the audition room, going for new projects. I'm living it up. I'm having fun right now. And I hope I can continue to work because it's a blessing and I love it.

ZAC MAKES HEADLINES!

Zac Efron is a media darling. You can't walk past a newsstand without seeing him grace the cover of magazines or newspapers. You can't turn on your TV or radio without hearing some report about his comings and goings. You can't check your computer homepage without seeing some insta-report on him or an entertainment site without noticing the thousands of bloggers who seem to be Zac-obsessed.

The simple fact is that Zac Efron makes news. Here are just a few of the headlines you may have seen throughout the years since he first hit the big and little screens.

⇨ Zac won the Teen Choice Break-out Star and Choice Chemistry (with Vanessa Hudgens) awards for *High School Musical* in 2006

➤ Zac and the cast of *Hairspray* won the Hollywood Film Award's "Ensemble of The Year" in 2007

⇨ Zac won the Young Hollywood Award's "One To Watch" for *Hairspray* in 2007

⇨ Zac won the Nickelodeon Kid's Choice Award's "Best Male Actor" in 2007

➤ **Zac won the Teen Choice Award's "Choice Male Hottie" in 2007**

⇨ Zac was included in In Touch's "10 Sexiest Guys" in Summer 2007

⇨ **Zac won the 9th Annual Family TV Award for "Best Actor" in *High School Musical* in 2007**

⇨ Zac was #1 on Teen magazine's 50 Hottest Guys in 2008

⇨ **Zac won the MTV Movie Award's "Breakthrough Performance" for *Hairspray* in 2008**

⇨ Zac won the 9th Annual Family TV Awards for "Best Actor" in *High School Musical* in 2007

⇨ **Zac was Yahoo's #1 Celebrity Search in 2006**

➤ Zac was included in People Magazine's 100 Most Beautiful People in 2007

⇨ **Zac graced the cover of Rolling Stone in August 2007**

⇨ Zac appeared in Vanessa's music video "Say OK!" in 2008

⇨ **Zac was included in Forbes magazine's Celebrity 100 List for 2008**

"I had no idea that anyone could ever care. That happens to, like, big stars. I woke up and my dad told me that I was in a newspaper on the beach—he made fun of me, he said I was 'frollicking.'" — *in response to tabloid headlines on his "Zanessa" sightings.*

BACK -IN-THE- DAY

Little Zac Efron . . . the boy from San Luis Obispo, CA, was special from the day he was born and not only to his family. He was singing and dancing from his toddler days, and his parents encouraged him to follow his talents—but early on all Zac wanted to do was play sports. Then, he tried out for a musical production, and a star was born. Check out what the early years were for Zac!

DADDY'S LITTLE BOY

Papa Dave remembers . . .

Baby Zac: **"He was a beautiful 'Gerber baby' with no hair and a perfect head. He cried if you left him alone and he loved to be held."**

Best Big Bro: "He's the big brother who is expected to be loving and nurturing. He's a good brother because he's not home much, and has a closet full of cool clothes and a fast computer in his room!"

Typical Kid: "Zac ate everything as a kid. He loved all the classic Disney movies, Teenage Mutant Ninja Turtles, and skateboarding."

17

High School English teacher Laura Wade recalls . . .

A Dedicated Student: "[Because of his Zac's acting] it was difficult for him to keep an 8-to-3 schedule. . . . What really impressed me was that he was able to follow through on all his assignments and never expected preferential treatment."

High School math teacher Jack Harris admits . . .

Math Wiz: "What took everyone else 50 minutes to learn, he tried to do in five. It was interesting to watch someone who really had a sponge-like capability to learn things."

Mr. Harris adds . . .

Equal Opportunity Pal: "In high school, Zac played sports. He was a man's man. He was the guy who really had his act together. Guys liked to hang out with him, but the girls seemed to be the ones who knew everything he was doing."

Middle School drama teacher Robyn Metchik remembers...

Superstar: "He had the looks and the talent! . . . We did *Music Man* and he played Harold Hill. He was very convincing and it was exciting to see that show come to life. The next year, we did *Nifty Fifties*, which is like an age-appropriate *Grease* musical. Because I always double-cast, he had two leading roles. One night he played the rock star, and the other he played the lead romantic jock. He *loved* the rock star part!"

Piano teacher Jeremy Mann says . . .

In The Stars: "The first time I met him, I said to myself, 'This kid's gonna grow up to be Brad Pitt.' He's probably the most charismatic little kid I've ever met."

The superstar looks back on his childhood days . . .

Role Model: "My role model growing up was Arnold Schwartzenegger, because he always played the cool superhero guy in all of his movies! . . . He's too cool, man."

Class Clown: "In my Spanish class, we had to write an essay about ourselves. So I wrote this fictional story about being raised by wolves and being brought to my hometown in a spaceship. My teacher got really mad and sent me to detention. I didn't know he was going to take it so seriously!"

Cool in School?: "Troy from *HSM* is a cool guy. He has this confidence that I didn't have in high school. I wouldn't say that I was a geek, but I was never one of the cool kids. I was too focused on school, and I was kind of known as one of the theater kids around town. I was also the shortest kid! I was really short and skinny until I got bigger in junior year, and I had a huge gap in my front teeth! I got teased about that gap more than anything else."

Theater Boy: "I wouldn't say you got flak about [being into theater in high school]. But I wouldn't say I got support either. My friends— it was all about skateboarding, sports. It was kind of like, 'Really? Like, really, you have fun acting? Dancing and singing? You really have fun doing that?'"

19

ZAC'S SUPER-DUPER PERSONAL PROFILE PRINTOUT!

EVERYTHING YOU NEED TO KNOW!

FULL NAME: Zachary David Alexander Efron

STAGE NAME: Zac Efron

NICKNAME: "A few of my friends back home call me 'Hollywood.'"

BIRTHDAY: October 18, 1987

BIRTHPLACE: San Luis Obispo, CA

HOME TOWN: Arroyo Grande, CA

CURRENT RESIDENCE: Los Angeles, CA

HEIGHT: 5' 10"

WEIGHT: 145 lbs

HAIR: Brown

EYES: Blue

PARENTS: Dave (an engineer at a power plant) and Starla Baskett (a former secretary who worked at the same power plant as her husband)

SIBLING: Younger brother Dylan

RIGHTY OR LEFTY: Righty

PETS: "Two dogs and a cat—the dogs [Australian shepherds] are Dreamer and Puppy. The cat [a Siamese] has like 20 names, but right now it's Simon."

HIGH SCHOOL: Arroyo Grande High School

MOST PRIZED POSSESSION: His Gibson guitar

GUILTY PLEASURE: Comic books and video games.

SECRET TALENT: Juggling

DREAM COSTARS: Christian Bale, Reese Witherspoon, Catherine Zeta-Jones

⇨ **As A Child:** "I loved Ninja Turtles and candy; I was terrified of girls, and I was always singing."

⇨ **At 13:** "I loved the theater and improv; getting good grades and definitely was not terrified of girls...."

⇨ **Present:** "Same as 13, but with the infinite knowledge that comes with graduating high school" [laughs]

FIRSTS

⇨ **Concert:** Wallflowers

⇨ **CD Bought:** *Aquabats* or *Spaceghost BBQ*

⇨ **Thing He Reaches for in the Refrigerator:** "Milk, or the Hershey's syrup, whatever is closer."

⇨ **Theme Park:** Disneyland

⇨ **Where He Went on His First Date:** The movies

⇨ **Song Played on Piano:** "Heart and Soul"

⇨ **Morning Routine:** Singing in the shower and then a jog

⇨ **Meal He Learned To Cook:** "The only dish I can pull off is ravioli. I made it from scratch the other day. It took me five hours, but it tasted really good!"

21

FAVES

- **Sports:** Baseball, basketball, surfing
- **Professional Sports Teams:** San Francisco Giants football team and Los Angeles Lakers basketball team
- **Sports Figure:** Kobe Bryant
- **TV Shows:** *American Idol*, *Survivor*, *Price Is Right*
- **Rerun TV Show:** "My favorite has always been *I Love Lucy*."
- **Movies:** *Goonies*, *Batman Begins*, the Bourne trilogy, *Die Hard*
- **Silly Movie:** *Superbad*
- **Singer:** Jack Johnson
- **Actors:** Brad Pitt, Christian Bale, Matt Damon, Al Pacino, and Jack Black
- **Old Time Actor:** Gene Kelly
- **Food:** Japanese
- **Fast Food:** Panda Express— Orange Chicken
- **Crackers:** Wheat Thins
- **Fruit:** Strawberries—"I love this strawberry that comes from a town near where I live. They are famous for their strawberries and, once a year, I go get a bunch of the most amazing strawberries I've had in my life. They're huge and so red on the inside and sweet. They remind me of summer."

- **Drink:** Milk
- **Candy:** Rice paper candy from Japan
- **Sandwiches:** Quiznos' honey mustard BBQ chicken sandwich, PB&J
- **Cereals:** Kashi, Granola, Honey Nut Cheerios, Quaker Oats
- **Ice Cream:** Cherry Garcia
- **Chewing Gum:** Orbit—"dark blue kind"
- **Diner:** Patty's in Toluca Lake, CA
- **Cologne:** Dolce & Gabana
- **Jewelry:** Dog tags
- **Accessory:** Gucci aviator sunglasses
- **Traveling Accessory:** Backpack
- **Footwear:** Sandals

- **Holiday:** Christmas—"Santa likes my cookies."

- **Family Vacation:** "Skiing in Oregon over Christmas."

- **City:** London

- **Dream Spot:** "Surfing at some white beach with clear water."

- **Color:** Blue

- **Tech Toy:** Cell phone

- **Latest Clothing Trend:** Checkered sneakers

- **Car:** Toyota Supra from *The Fast and the Furious*

- **Collection:** "My autographed baseball collection. I've got almost every player from the Giants for the past 10 years."

- **Superhero:** Spiderman

- **iPod Downloads:** "You Are Not Alone" by Michael Jackson, "Weapon of Choice" by Fat Boy Slim, "Chasing Cars" by Snow Patrol, "Boston" by Augustana, and "Digital Love" by Daft Punk.

SCHOOL DAYS

- **Fave Subject:** English—"there's never one right answer!"

- **Least Fave Subject:** AP Chemistry—"I got straight A's, but it was really hard."

- **Math Tips:** "A calculator is your best friend."

- **Fave Science Subject:** Biology

- **Science Meltdown:** "I spilled sulfuric acid on my notebook—my entire year's notes melted instantly."

- **Language Studied in School:** Spanish

- **Fave Historical Era Studied:** "The 40s and 50s."

- **Best Thing About School:** "Seeing my friends"

- **Worst Thing About School:** "Waking up in the morning."

- **Fave Teacher:** "Robyn Metchik—she taught drama in Middle School. I've never had so much fun."

ON·THE·SET WITH ZAC

Zac invites you behind the cameras on his movie and TV sets!

Derby Stallion—Patrick McCardle
(Feature Film)

"I assumed when I signed on for this movie that the horseback riding was all going to be done by stuntmen, which is good because I'd never done any horseback riding. Then the first day when I came on the set, and talked to one of the producers, he said, 'Yes, you have three lessons and you're going to be jumping.' I guess that really turned on my adrenaline. I started focusing 24/7 on horseback riding. They had one of the greatest teachers come in and help me."

Summerland—
Cameron Bale
(TV Series)

"I went in [for the audition] and two weeks later they gave me a role. I think it was a great way to break into working. Previously all I had done was guest spots and pilots, and things that never went through. . . . I really got the chance to build a family with the people at *Summerland*. I would see them three days a week and I got to feel what it was like [to do a TV series]."

Miracle Run—Steven Morgan
(TV Movie)

"I was so happy to get that role [of an autistic twin]. I came in last minute and it was one of the very last auditions. Right after I did the audition, I got the call and they asked me to do the movie. So within the next day or two, I flew out and began shooting in Louisiana. It was amazing and the whole way there I read a book on autism and how the world looks through their eyes. It was actually a great book called *Thinking in Pictures*. After I read a few chapters and was more educated on autism, I tried to just think about how each scene would go through their eyes. That's something every actor does; it's what you've got to do. I added a few mannerisms that I patented and that was it. The movie was a blast to shoot and the guy who played opposite me, Bubba Lewis, is a good friend of mine to this day, so I made some good relationships on that film."

High School Musical—Troy Bolton
(TV Movie)

"It was amazing. It was a dream to be able to sing and dance, and play basketball and act all in the same project. I got thrown into the mix and immediately I was off and running and practicing constantly for this role. We had so much fun. . . . I'm not much of a dancer. It took a lot of Gatorade and aspirin to get me through dancing and basketball rehearsals. . . . We showed up to Utah two weeks before the movie started shooting. We weren't really educated as to why we were showing up two weeks early and little did we know that they had two solid weeks of nine to six o'clock rehearsals planned for us—long hours of just dance rehearsals and basketball practice and then working on scenes. It was like boot camp. It was incredible. I don't know how I made it through. I had so many muscle pulls and shin splints, and everyone in that movie were troopers. . . . I learned so much on *High School Musical*, working with Kenny [Ortega] and the choreographers. We did so much dancing, it really got me back into shape."

High School Musical 2— Troy Bolton (TV Movie)

"The scene that was most fun? I had a lot of fun days on the golf course. I had a few romantic scenes between Troy and Gabriella on the golf course. I did not fake kissing!"

Hairspray—Link Larkin
(Feature Film)

"Link brings the cool element. He's the kind of character that leaves people thinking, 'He's my favorite!' He's shallow and not that smart—that's the fun of him. . . . It was a real treat to work with John Travolta. I'd been watching John since *Grease*. It was one of the first musicals I remember seeing. I was a huge fan of his character and the whole movie. This guy has been in my life for so long and it was so surreal to actually meet him. . . . I love Queen Latifah's work. She's an inspiration everywhere. And she's so sweet. She's just a great person. She's very fun to be around. She can brighten up any room. . . . Nikki Blonsky is amazing. . . . Amanda Bynes is a great girl. From the second we met, the whole cast meshed. . . . The younger ones in the cast—me, Elijah, Brittany, Nikki, and Amanda—we all stuck together a lot and got to know each other well. We had our own little posse. . . . A funny *Hairspray* secret? The hairspray that we used in the film is not hairspray at all. In order to get it to read on camera, it was anti-perspirant deodorant spray. In some of the songs in the movie we were constantly spraying hairspray on ourselves, around ourselves, so by the end of a take we would have completely covered ourselves, saturated our skin and our hair in deodorant. We had to wash it all out."

High School Musical 3: Senior Year— Troy Bolton (Feature Film)

"I felt like the first two movies all over again. We just kind of can't go wrong with Kenny Ortega as our director and leader, and our great cast and crew. We've got no squabbles to get through. . . . Everything's been stepped up a few notches, all the dances, and I think the songs are pretty catchy this time around. And it's our senior year, so we've got graduation and prom to look forward to. All fun things to have in a movie."

17 Again—Mike O'Donnell (Feature Film)

"I play Mike O'Donnell. Mike is not thrilled with the way his life has turned out. In the beginning he had all these opportunities, so many ways he could take his life, but in one day during high school that's all stripped from him. So he wishes he could go back to that day in his life where everything came crashing down. He wants to go re-live that and maybe play it differently. The idea of being able to go back to high school with the knowledge that you have as a 37-year-old— that excited me from day one. . . . I could just go off and play a kid anywhere. The idea that drew me to this role was that it's a different thing playing a 37-year-old-guy. . . . I'm essentially playing an old, kind of depressed middle-aged man."

Me and Orson Welles— Richard Samuels (Feature Film)

"He gets swept into this amazing adventure and in a way becomes Orson Welles' protégé. It's just a very, very fun coming-of-age story. . . . It's a completely different project than I've ever done before. Gosh, I would say that's the main reason I'm looking forward to doing [it]. It's just a side I've never really shown before. I think it's going to be a lot of color in this movie. A lot of things you haven't seen before, hopefully. I'm crossing my fingers, anyway."

ZAC'S
TOP 10 SECRETS

SHHHH! DON'T TELL!

⇨ **The most embarrassing hairstyle I ever had was when . . .** "I dyed [my hair] silver like Sisqó [the singer] in 'Thong Song'."

⇨ **When I was growing up I had a poster of . . .** "Tyra Banks—it was on the ceiling above my bunk bed."

⇨ **Zac's secret talent is . . .** "Hacky Sack! The other day, traffic was completely stopped, so I got out of my car and played Hacky Sack for half-an-hour."

⇨ **Zac's idol is . . .** "John Travolta. He's too cool, man. . . . When I met him I was shaking in my boots. I learned about professionalism from him."

⇨ **In school Zac was a member of**

. . . the acting team called Destination Imagination

Zac's grandmother was a circus performer . . . Not! — "I actually found out that was sort of a fib on my part, because she wasn't in the circus. She was in some kind of traveling group, but not the circus. The picture I found was just her on Halloween and my mom educated me about that after she read it in an interview."

Zac shark attack . . . "I was surfing, and the waves were all closing in on us and killing us, and rocks were coming up from the ground and hitting us. All of a sudden I feel a huge brush up against my leg and immediately I think 'shark,' because we had recently had a shark attack at Pismo beach. So I am freaking out! It was a long stroke too, not when you touch seaweed that brushes against you and sticks. This was a huge brush along me, and it was hard and it moved me! I was like, 'Oh my god, a shark is underneath me!' I come up and get on my board and I am so scared I can't even speak. It's like my life is flashing before me eyes and I start to paddle in. All of a sudden I hear my friend laughing and I turn around, and a seal is about halfway out of the water looking at me. I was like, 'Oh my god!' and I lean back on my board and my heart slowly stopped beating. I thought it was going to jump out of my chest, and the seal is just sitting there laughing at me and looking at me. It was pretty funny."

Piano-man and guitar-player Zac also plays another instrument . . . "I played the clarinet in band in high school."

Zac goes scissors snippy . . . When Zac was in fifth grade, his dad recalls, "He accidentally cut off one of his eyebrows—He decided to try to make the other one match. He got really teased about that by his classmates."

Zac still goes home to mom on laundry day . . . "I don't make it long without my mom cooking for me or doing my laundry."

⇨ Zac loves Leo! . . . "He's kind of my definition of teen star because when I was growing up his face was everywhere. I think since then he's developed an incredible body of work. If there's anyone I'd like to emulate it's him."

⇨ Idol Worship . . . Zac says the most famous person in his phone is actor Ian McKellen, one of his all time favorites.

⇨ Vanessa-Phone . . . Zac has Vanessa's picture as the background on his iPhone!

ZAC CHAT...
HEARD IN THE HALLWAY

CHECK OUT WHAT HIS FRIENDS HAVE TO SAY!

Known as one of Hollywood's good guys, you never see Zac's name in the tabloid headlines. His friends, family, and fans tell you why!

Michelle Trachtenberg, costar in *17 Again*:
"Zac is adorable. And you know what? He's so not affected. He's like the loveliest thing and doing a great job in the movie. We are really proud of him . . . He's really humble, which is nice. He gets me [candy as] presents."

Dave Efron, father:
"I'm proud of his approach to acting, remaining grounded despite his success, excelling academically, and being accepted to UCLA. It's a good feeling to be referred to as 'Zac's Dad.'"

Perez Hilton, gossip blogger:
"I think he's still living in the same apartment complex, and he still hangs out in the same places. He's been able to keep a level head above the masses."

John Travolta, costar in *Hairspray*:
"Zac is very talented. He reminds me of me in *Grease*."

Gary March, Entertainment President, Disney Channel:
"Zac radiates this sense of attainability—as if anyone who meets him can be his friend. That's not something you learn in acting class. That's something you're born with."

Vanessa Hudgens, costar in *High School Musical* and girlfriend:
"My first impression? Ooh la la! . . . He's an amazing guy!"

Amanda Bynes, costar in *Hairspray*:
"Zac's a really nice guy, but he's more like a brother to me. He's definitely a completely normal teenage boy!"

Monique Coleman, costar in *High School Musical*:
"Zac has a way of wooing women by including them. By making every single girl feel like they could be his girlfriend."

ZACALICIOUS CRUSHIN'
!!!Love Notes!!!

Kissy Kissy!

➪ "My first kiss was in a tree fort. . . . I don't recall if it was in fourth or fifth grade, but it was in a tree fort."

➪ His first real kiss was in 7th grade during a game of Truth or Dare.

Best Girl Friend B-day Present

➪ "Chocolate."

Heartthrob Idol

➪ "It's very fun. I have the best fans in the world! They are the most excited and supportive fans on the planet. I'm very grateful, just to see how happy they are about [my movies]. It's a real treat. I love them!"

Dating Do's & Don'ts

➪ "I like girls who laugh a lot and are spontaneous. I don't like a girl who hides her face with tons of makeup."

Dating Advice To His Younger Brother

⇨ "Let the girls come to you!"

Love At First Sight

⇨ "I don't know if I believe in love at first sight, but of course I believe in two people having chemistry right away. A girl should be really easy to talk to. When I lose track of time because we've been talking, I think that's really fun."

Miss Right

⇨ "I like energetic, happy-go-lucky girls—when everything comes together to make the whole package."

Flipper

⇨ "When I was in the fourth grade, everyone would do backflips off the swing set. One time, to impress a girl, I decided to do a double backflip. So the swing was going and I was up really high (probably the highest I had ever been), and when I got about one and a half times around, I landed right on my butt. It hurt so bad and it was really embarrassing."

Be Yourself

⇨ "You have to be yourself. A lot of times—and even I do this—when I'm in front of a girl I like, I put on a show, and that doesn't work. You realize that once you stop doing that, the girl really likes you best."

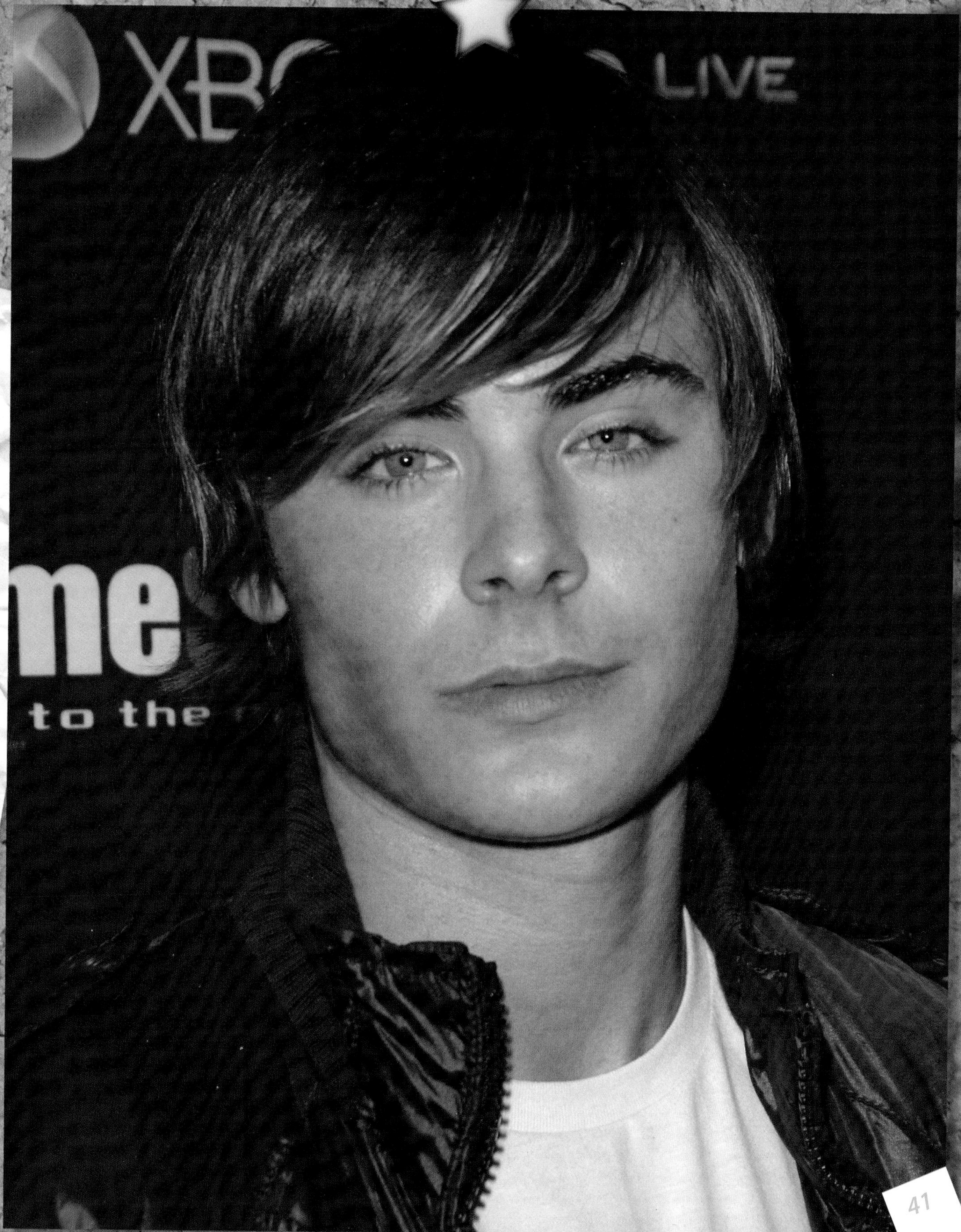
XBO
LIVE
me
to the

ZAC'S ADDRESS BOOK

How To Get In Touch With Him . . . From E-Mail To Snail-Mail

Information Web sites for Zac Efron

En.wikipedia.org/wiki/Zac_Efron

www.imdb.com

www.hairspraymovie.com

http://tv.disney.go.com/disneychannel/original movies/highschoolmusical/

http://tv.disney.go.com/disneychannel/original movies/highschoolmusical2/

http://tv.disney.go.com/disneychannel/original movies/highschoolmusical3/

Mail Addresses

Zac Efron
c/o High School Musical
Disney Channel
3800 West Alameda Ave.
Burbank, CA 91505

Zac Efron
c/o CAA
2000 Avenue of the Stars
Los Angeles, CA 90067

Zac Efron
c/o Baker Winokur Ryder Public
Relations
5700 Wilshire Blvd.
Suite 550
Los Angeles, CA 90036

!!!ALERT!!!

AS OF THE TIME WE WENT TO PRESS, ZAC DOES NOT HAVE HIS OWN PERSONAL MYSPACE ACCOUNT. ZAC ALSO DOES NOT HAVE A XANGA, BEBO, ANY ONLINE JOURNALS, OR OTHER BLOGS. ANY ONLINE COMMUNITY THAT CLAIMS TO HAVE AN OFFICIAL ZAC EFRON PROFILE IS NOT REAL.

TRIPICTURES

QUIZ WIZ

How Well Do You Know Zac?

CHOOSE THE RIGHT ANSWER

1. Zac's weirdest talent is . . .

    (a) wiggling his right ear

    (b) blowing spit bubbles

    (c) singing like Mickey Mouse

2. The game Zac loves to play with his younger brother is . . .

    (a) tic-tac-toe

    (b) Sudoku

    (c) golf

3. Zac has a sports tradition with his dad . . .

    (a) going to San Francisco Giants baseball games two hours early to catch batting practice

    (b) diving off cliffs in Mexico

    (c) running with the bulls in Spain

4. Zac used to drive an old Oldsmobile given to him by his grandpa—he traded that in for . . .

    (a) an Audi

    (b) a Hummer

    (c) a 10-speed racing bike

5. When he was a kid, Zac used to fight with his little brother Dylan over . . .

    (a) riding in the front seat of the car

    (b) Playstation

    (c) who would feed the dogs

FILL IN THE BLANK—FINISH THE SENTENCE

1. Zac's favorite traveling accessory is a _____.
2. Zac's favorite holiday is _____.
3. Zac's nickname is _____.
4. Zac played the _____ in his high school band.
5. Zac played the character _____ in the movie *17 Again*.
6. Zac's favorite fast food restaurant is _____.

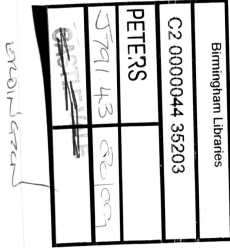

Zac Efron is the hottest up-and-coming young actor around and you can read all about him in this glossy, full-colored scrapbook! 48 pages packed with facts, Zac's answers to some of your biggest questions, quotes from friends and family, and, of course, lots of full-page pictures! Get all the info on this amazing talent.

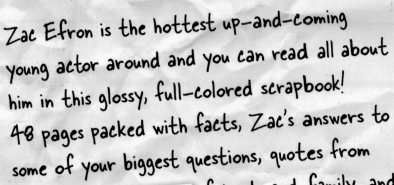

■ SCHOLASTIC
www.scholastic.com

$5.99 US
$7.50 CA
£3.99 UK

ISBN-13: 978-0-545-11414-1
ISBN-10: 0-545-11414-4

50599

EAN

9 780545 114141